Zoe's Rescue
ZOO

With special thanks to Natalie Doherty

To Theo

Text Copyright © 2017 by Hothouse Fiction
Illustrations Copyright © 2017 by Sophy Williams

ISBN 978-1-338-19448-7

10 9 8 7 6 5 4 3   19 20 21 22

Printed in the U.S.A.   40
This edition first printing 2018

The Scruffy Sea Otter

Amelia Cobb

Illustrated by Sophy Williams

Scholastic Inc.

Chapter One
A Monday Morning Mystery

Brrrriiing! Brrrriiing!

Zoe Parker's eyes flew open as the telephone rang downstairs. It was still very early in the morning, and Zoe could tell from the dim light coming through her curtains that the sun hadn't totally come up yet.

1

"Who's calling so early?" she mumbled, rubbing her eyes.

Usually on school days, Zoe was woken by the sound of Oscar the African elephant trumpeting noisily in his enclosure! That was because Zoe lived somewhere very special: the Rescue Zoo.

The Rescue Zoo was an amazing place where animals who had no home or who were lost or hurt could find a safe place to live. Zoe's great-uncle, Horace Higgins, had started the zoo several years ago. He was a famous animal expert and explorer, and he was off on one of his adventures around the world right now.

Zoe's mom, Lucy, was the Rescue Zoo's vet, and she and Zoe lived in a cozy little cottage on the edge of the zoo. This meant that Zoe could visit the animals any time she wanted! Zoe thought she was the luckiest girl in the world to live where she did. She loved animals more than anything!

As the telephone continued to ring, Zoe heard her mom's bedroom door creak open and footsteps pad downstairs. "Hello?" she heard her mom say sleepily.

Suddenly, Zoe had a thought. "Meep, are you awake?" she whispered anxiously. "I hope one of the animals isn't sick!"

Zoe knew that the night zookeepers would call her mom in an animal emergency, no matter what time it was, so that her mom could rush out and help.

There was silence for a moment. Then, at the foot of the bed, next to Zoe's toes, the comforter wriggled. A little furry face with big golden eyes popped out!

Meep was a gray mouse lemur with soft fur and a long curly tail. He was Zoe's best friend and he lived in the cottage with Zoe and her mom. Zoe and Meep did everything together—including talking!

On her sixth birthday, Zoe had realized that she could understand animals' grunts, barks, and roars, and speak back to them too. It had made living in the Rescue Zoo even more fun! Zoe had always kept this a secret from other people though—even her mom.

Meep's pointy ears were pricked up so that he could listen to what Zoe's mom was saying. Zoe knew that lemurs had excellent hearing—much better than humans'! "I think she's laughing, Zoe!" he chirped.

To Zoe's relief, she realized that Meep was right. She could hear now that her mom was chatting happily with whoever was on the other end of the telephone. That must mean that none of the animals were hurt or ill. "So what do you think's going on, Meep?" she wondered.

Meep's ears twitched. "She's coming back up the stairs now," he squeaked. "Maybe we'll find out!"

Zoe heard footsteps on the stairs again,

and a moment later there was a gentle
tap on Zoe's bedroom door.

"Zoe, are you awake?" her mom
asked, popping her head inside the room.
Zoe and her mom had the same dark
curly hair. Her mom was beaming with
excitement. "I've got a surprise for you!"
she said. "Quick, hop out of bed and
come with me."

"What is it? Where are we going?"
asked Zoe, climbing out of bed.

"You'll see!" replied her mom. "Put
some clothes on and meet me downstairs."

Zoe stared as her mom disappeared
back into her own bedroom, humming
cheerily. "This is so weird!" she whispered
to Meep as she quickly put on some
clothes and laced up her sneakers.

Meep jumped from the bed and perched

on her shoulder. "I'm coming too!" he chattered eagerly.

Zoe and Meep were waiting by the front door when Zoe's mom appeared. Mrs. Parker smiled when she saw them. "Let's go!" she said, ushering them outside and locking the door behind them.

"Where are we going?" Zoe asked again. "What's happening?"

"You'll find out very soon, I promise," her mom assured her.

To Zoe's surprise, her mom walked toward the jeep that was parked around the side of the cottage and got in.

Zoe climbed into the jeep and strapped herself in, with Meep nestling in her lap. Her mom started the engine and they began to drive slowly through the zoo. The early morning sun was casting a warm light over the flowerbeds bursting with spring flowers and the tall rooftops of Higgins Hall. This was the huge manor house that had belonged to Great-Uncle Horace's family for years and years, and was now home to some of the Rescue Zoo's reptiles.

Lots of the animals were beginning to
stir as Zoe and her mom drove along.
The giraffes were stretching out their long
necks, just like Zoe always stretched her
arms in the morning, and the hippos were
plodding into their mud bath for an early-

morning dip. But Zoe spotted the owls
cuddling together on a branch in their
enclosure with their eyes starting to close.
Most owls were nocturnal animals,
just like bats, which meant they slept
through the daytime instead of at night.

Zoe smiled as Rory, the little lion cub, yawned widely and stretched out his paws before nudging his friend Leonard awake. As the jeep rumbled past the lions' enclosure, Zoe saw Rory stare at them in surprise and growl curiously. The little cub wanted to know where Zoe was off to in the early hours of the morning— almost as much as Zoe herself did!

"I love seeing the zoo like this!" Zoe said. "It's so quiet without any visitors."

Her mom nodded. "This is one of my favorite times of day too, when the only people around are the zookeepers."

Just as she said this, Zoe spotted Jess, the otter-keeper, walking along the path in the direction of the otter enclosure. Her blonde hair was tied back in a braid, and she was carrying a big red bucket of fish.

"Jess must be about to give the otters their breakfast!" Zoe said, waving.

They drove right through the zoo and out of the gates, which were carved from wood and showed lots of different animals. Zoe frowned as she noticed which road her mom was taking them down. "We're heading toward the river!" she realized.

"That's right," said her mom, grinning.

Zoe was beginning to feel very excited— and *very* curious!

The jeep turned a corner, and as the river came into view, Zoe saw a boat in the distance, sailing toward them. It was bright red, with a yellow sail fluttering in the breeze. Painted on the sail was a symbol: a colorful hot air balloon. Zoe could make out a figure standing at the wheel, with a head of messy white hair. As she watched, the figure raised an arm and waved.

Zoe stared. "That's the Rescue Zoo boat!" she cried. "And . . . that's Great-Uncle Horace! He's back!"

Chapter Two
First Mate Zoe!

Zoe bounced up and down impatiently as the boat drifted toward them. When she couldn't wait any longer, she scooped Meep into her arms, raced to the river's edge, and began waving her arms. "Great-Uncle Horace!" she shouted excitedly.

Chuckling, her mom joined her. "It was

Great-Uncle Horace on the phone this morning!" she explained. "He thought this would be a fun surprise."

The boat drew closer to the riverbank and Zoe saw Great-Uncle Horace throw out a long rope, which her mom caught and wrapped tightly around a wooden post. Great-Uncle Horace was wearing a tattered, stripy sailor's sweater and a blue captain's hat, and his white beard looked even wilder than usual. "All aboard!" he called, beaming as the boat bumped against the bank. "Take my hand, First Mate Zoe, and hop on!"

Zoe reached out her hand, grabbed Great-Uncle Horace's, and jumped aboard the boat, with her mom just behind her. The deck felt strange and wobbly underneath her feet, and she had

to take a few steps to find her balance.
Meep squealed
anxiously and
scrambled onto
her shoulder,
wrapping
his long tail
around her
neck to make
sure he didn't
fall off.

"Great-
Uncle
Horace, I've
really missed
you!" Zoe cried,
jumping into his arms for
a hug. "You were gone for so long
this time."

"And I'm so happy to be home, Zoe!"

Great-Uncle Horace replied warmly.
"I've been on such an adventure.
I've been to Russia! It's such a vast
country, full of huge mountains, wild
forests—and lots of different animals
that needed my help! Isn't that right,
Kiki?"

There was a squawk as a blue bird
fluttered down from the flagpole and
landed on Great-Uncle Horace's
shoulder. Kiki was a hyacinth macaw
with beautiful glossy feathers, bright
beady eyes, and a curved beak. Great-
Uncle Horace had rescued her when
she was only an egg, and she'd stayed
with him ever since.

"It's been a long journey back!"
continued Great-Uncle Horace,
stroking Kiki fondly.

"Did you find an animal who needed

a place to live?" asked Zoe hopefully. Whenever Great-Uncle Horace came across an animal that couldn't stay in the wild anymore, he brought it back to the Rescue Zoo. Zoe's mind whirled as she thought about some of the creatures that had arrived at the zoo recently: a gorgeous family of arctic wolves; a pair of playful panda cubs; a fluffy baby polar bear. If Great-Uncle Horace *had* brought a new animal back this time, what would it be?

Great-Uncle Horace laughed. "I certainly did, Zoe," he replied. "Not just one animal—but *three*! Take a look inside that crate."

Zoe turned and saw a large wooden crate tucked securely at the back of the boat. She stepped toward it and peered

through a gap between the wooden
boards. All she could make out were three
sets of dark, shining eyes. On her shoulder,
Meep gave an excited squeak.

"I can't tell what they are!" Zoe cried.

"Let me give you a clue," said Great-
Uncle Horace. "These animals are
mammals, but they spend lots of time in
the water."

Zoe bit her lip and thought. "Polar bears?" she guessed. "Or maybe . . . seals!"

Great-Uncle Horace shook his head and gave a big smile. "They're sea otters!" he explained. "Baby otters are called pups, just like baby seals. There are two sisters and one brother. I'm afraid they were orphaned when Russian hunters captured their parents—sea otters are often hunted for their fur, which means they are an endangered species, sadly. So we'll give them a nice, safe home at the Rescue Zoo."

"Otters!" said Zoe. "Like Otto and Benedict?"

"Well, Otto and Benedict are *river* otters, my dear," Great-Uncle Horace explained. "But these are *sea* otters. They need to live in salt water, not freshwater. I've already

sent a message to Jess, asking her to
prepare a special area with a saltwater
pool for our new arrivals to play in. I
asked her to keep it a secret!"

"Jess *has* seemed very busy this week—
and very mysterious!" said Zoe's mom,
laughing. "Now I know why."

"I bet that's where she was going when
we saw her this morning—the new
enclosure!" Zoe realized. "She'll be so
excited to have three new baby otters to
take care of."

"Let's set off for the zoo right away,"
said Great-Uncle Horace. "Our new
arrivals have traveled a long way, and
they'll be tired and hungry. Perhaps you
could help me with the crate, Lucy?"

Zoe jumped off the boat and watched
as Great-Uncle Horace and her mom

carefully lifted the crate off the boat and carried it to the back of the jeep. On the drive back to the zoo, Zoe listened to the snuffles and squeaks from inside the crate. While her mom and Great-Uncle Horace were busy chatting in the front, she twisted around and whispered quietly, "Don't worry—we're going somewhere really nice. I think you'll like it."

Once they reached the zoo, Zoe's mom parked the jeep right outside the new enclosure and they all jumped out. Jess was waiting by the gate, smiling. "Good morning!" she called. "Welcome back, Mr. Higgins. I got your message about the new enclosure, and it's all ready. I can't wait to meet the pups!"

"I think that makes two of you!" replied Great-Uncle Horace, winking at Zoe,

who was grinning
excitedly.

The grown-ups
lifted the crate
out of the jeep,
while Zoe
opened the
gate using
the necklace
she always wore.
It was a silver chain
with a charm shaped like
a paw print, which contained a
special chip that opened all the gates and
doors in the Rescue Zoo.

It had been her best-ever birthday present
from Great-Uncle Horace, and Zoe loved
it. She held the gate wide open as the
crate was carried inside and set down.

"You've done a marvelous job, Jess!" exclaimed Great-Uncle Horace, and Jess gave him a big smile. Zoe thought so too. There was a clear pool, with lots of big wooden logs piled up around the edges, and even some wooden ramps and slides for the otters to play on. Dotted around the edge of the enclosure were tall, leafy trees that offered plenty of shade from the sunshine. Waiting at the side of the pool was the red bucket Zoe had seen Jess carrying that morning, filled with shiny fish for the otters to eat, and a pile of colorful balls and other toys. "The water is the perfect temperature for sea otters, and there's just the right level of salt for them," Jess explained.

Zoe's mom unbuckled the straps on the crate and gently lowered one side.

Zoe held her breath as high-pitched squeaks came from inside the crate, and then a black snout appeared, sniffing the air. Next came a pale furry head with whiskers and big, alert black eyes, followed by a sleek, dark body. The otter looked around at the enclosure, squeaked happily, and trotted out of the crate.

"That's the oldest female," explained Great-Uncle Horace.

"She's so cute—and so small!" whispered Zoe.

A second otter followed right after the first. "And that's her twin brother," added Great-Uncle Horace. "Otter twins are very rare, Zoe. I've never met a pair before. We're very lucky to have them! They're around a year old, I think."

Finally, a third tiny face popped out

of the crate, glancing around shyly. This baby was even smaller than her sister and brother. Zoe gasped as the little otter scampered out. She had bright eyes and scruffy, tufty brown fur sticking up in all directions. Zoe thought the otter was one of the cutest things she'd ever seen! "That's the youngest pup, another female," Great-Uncle Horace explained. "Just four months old! And she's a little bit more nervous, so we'll need to make her feel extra welcome."

Zoe watched as the two older otters headed straight for the edge of the water. "Oh no! What if they jump right in?" she said anxiously. "Will they be OK?"

"Don't worry, Zoe," Great-Uncle Horace reassured her. "Baby otters are born knowing how to swim."

The otter twins plunged into the water, gliding underneath the surface before popping their heads back up and squeaking excitedly. Their little sister paused at the edge of the pool, watching them eagerly, although she didn't look as though she felt quite ready to follow them. *As soon as she's settled in, I bet she'll be*

jumping in right after them! Zoe thought.

"They love the water, don't they?" said her mom, smiling as the twins splashed and ducked.

Zoe giggled. It seemed as though the new arrivals were feeling at home already!

Chapter Three
Zoe's Special Task

As Great-Uncle Horace, Zoe's mom, and
Jess chatted about the otters' diet and
what special supplies Jess would need, Zoe
crouched down by the edge of the pool.
She wanted to say hello to the otters and
explain that she was there to help them
with any problems or questions—and
she was eager to become friends too!

While the grown-ups were distracted, she decided to take her chance.

"I'm Zoe," she whispered, smiling at the twin otter pups, who looked at her curiously and then swam toward her. "I live here at the zoo, in a little cottage close by—my mom's the zoo vet, so her job is to take care of animals. And Meep lives here too. He's a gray mouse lemur and my best friend," she added.

Meep gave a friendly wave. "Hello! Welcome to the zoo," he chattered.

"What are your names?" asked Zoe.

The twins squealed playfully, their eyes bright. "So you're Nina and you're Alex," repeated Zoe. "But how can I tell you apart? You look so alike."

Nina squeaked and waved a furry paw in the air, and Zoe spotted a patch of pale fur. Glancing at Alex, Zoe saw that her twin brother didn't have this extra marking, and nodded. "That's a good way to tell you apart!" she said. "And what's your name?" she added, smiling at the twins' little sister.

Shyly, the tiny otter squeaked her name. "Sasha! What a pretty name," said Zoe. "Meep and I really hope you like your new home."

The twins squeaked eagerly, but Zoe thought Sasha looked a little bit bewildered. "Don't worry, Sasha. This is a really nice place to live," Zoe whispered, reaching out to stroke the pup. Unlike her sleeker sister and brother, Sasha's fur was tufty and fluffy, and stuck up messily. Zoe thought she was so sweet!

Before she could say anything else,

Great-Uncle Horace, Jess, and her mom
walked over to join her. "Aren't they
fascinating creatures!" said Great-Uncle
Horace, beaming. "Did you know, Zoe,
that otters have the thickest fur in the

whole animal kingdom? Unfortunately, that's why they're a target for hunters— their coats are wonderfully warm. They're very smart animals too; sea otters often use tools like pebbles or rocks to open shellfish, just as we might use a can opener to open a can!"

"Have you thought of names for them yet, Zoe?" her mom asked.

Zoe smiled. She always tried to find out a new animal's name when it arrived at the zoo. Then, because she couldn't tell anyone that she had spoken to the animal, she often pretended she had thought of the name herself! "I thought we could call the twins Nina and Alex," she suggested shyly. "Nina has a light mark on one of her paws, so we can tell which twin is which. And can we call the little one Sasha?"

"I think those names are perfect," said her mom.

Just as she said this, Sasha wriggled her body determinedly and plunged into the water with a splash. "She must have decided it was safe to give it a try!" Zoe's mom laughed.

Zoe watched as Sasha paddled after her brother and sister, but she wasn't as fast as them and was struggling to keep up, despite squeaking hopefully at them to wait for her. The twins were floating on their backs close together, with their paws clasped, and they didn't seem to notice their little sister. Great-Uncle Horace saw Zoe's anxious face and smiled reassuringly. "The twins have a very close bond," he explained. "That means their little sister

might get left out sometimes—but there's
no need to worry, Zoe. We've just been
discussing how to make sure she settles in
just as well as her big sister and brother."

Jess nodded. "Because the otters are so young, I'll need to help encourage them to learn the important skills their mom would have shown them in the wild," she explained. "Things like using tools, diving for food, and becoming even better, faster swimmers. Sasha will need extra time and attention though, because she's the smallest. So every day, I'll spend a few hours helping her, until she can keep up with the twins."

Zoe's hand shot in the air. She didn't even have to think it over—she already knew this was something she wanted to assist with if she could! "Can I help?" she pleaded. "I can come before school and after school and on the weekends. Please?"

Jess smiled at her. "Thank you, Zoe. That would be great!" she replied. "You're so good at helping new animals feel at home here. In fact, your job could be to take special care of Sasha—if your mom doesn't mind."

"I don't mind at all," answered Zoe's mom, smiling. "As long as you do all your homework first, Zoe. And you must do exactly as Jess tells you, especially when you're around the water."

Zoe nodded. She felt so proud—and so excited too! "Can I start this afternoon?" she asked hopefully.

"Of course! Just come and find me when you get home from school," Jess replied.

"Speaking of school, we'd better get you back to the cottage so you can have breakfast and put on your uniform," her mom added.

"And I must be off too," explained Great-Uncle Horace. He caught the look of disappointment on Zoe's face and added quickly, "Not for very long, I promise! But I've heard about some special swans a little farther down the river and I'd love to see them. I'm going to sail my boat to where they're nesting. I'll be back at the zoo in a few days."

"And we've got a busy week ahead anyway, haven't we, Zoe?" her mom added as Zoe ran to give Great-Uncle Horace a hug. "Come on, now—let's go. I promise you can come back later!"

"See you soon!" called Zoe, waving at Jess as she and her mom jumped back into the jeep.

As they drove back toward the cottage, with Meep cuddled in Zoe's lap, Zoe felt a huge grin spreading across her face. She couldn't wait to spend more time with the adorable baby otters!

Chapter Four
Zoe's Special Visitors

"Mom, I'm home!" called Zoe, rushing into the cottage that afternoon. She had spent the whole day at school thinking about the baby otters and telling her friends and teacher about them. She was so excited about getting home and heading straight for their enclosure!

Zoe pulled her book bag off her

shoulders, but then noticed two pairs of shoes that she didn't recognize in the rack by the front door. There were some fancy red high heels and a small pair of sandals with a daisy pattern on them. *Of course—Auntie Carol and Olivia are here!* thought Zoe, smiling. *That's what Mom meant when she said we had a busy few days ahead. I completely forgot that they were coming to stay!*

Hearing voices in the kitchen, Zoe ran through the door. Auntie Carol was sitting at the table with a cup of coffee, chatting with her mom. She had dark hair cut in a short bob and wore red reading glasses. Zoe's little cousin Olivia sat on her knee, her hair in pigtails, clutching a very threadbare teddy bear in her tiny hands. Meep was perched by the fruit bowl, sneakily helping himself to a banana.

"Zoe!" cried Auntie Carol, smiling. "How's my favorite niece? Olivia's been so excited to see you."

"Hi, Auntie Carol!" said Zoe, rushing over to hug them both. "Hi, Olivia. When did you get here?"

"At lunchtime," explained Auntie Carol. "And we seem to have picked a good week to come. Your mom's been telling us all about your new sea otters—how exciting! I hear you're going to be taking special care of the littlest one."

"I thought we could all walk over to the otter enclosure together, before dinner," Zoe's mom suggested.

"That would be great!" said Zoe. She grinned at her little cousin. "Do you like animals, Olivia?"

Olivia beamed back and nodded enthusiastically. Zoe thought Olivia was *almost* as cute as the baby otters she'd met that morning, with her big blue eyes and smiley face. "I like Meep best!" Olivia told Zoe. "I want to hug him!"

Zoe giggled as Meep grumbled to himself. Olivia was only three years old, and the last time she and Auntie Carol had visited, she had squeezed poor Meep so tightly that he'd scampered upstairs to Zoe's bedroom and hidden under the bed until their visitors left.

Zoe quickly went to change out of her school uniform into jeans and a T-shirt, and then they all walked through the zoo together. Zoe and her mom pointed out different animals to Auntie Carol and Olivia along the way. "Those are the

emperor penguins.
Look at the
funny way they
waddle along!"
Zoe told her
little cousin, who
jumped up and
down excitedly, her
teddy still clutched
in her hands. "And

the giraffes are over there. Their necks
are really long, aren't they?"

"Eddie wants to see too," Olivia told
her, holding her teddy bear out.

Zoe took the teddy and lifted him up
high, as if to peer over the fence, before
returning him to Olivia. Auntie Carol and
her mom chuckled. "I bought Eddie for
Olivia before she was even born," Auntie

Carol explained, nodding at the bear.
"He's a very special bear. He comes
everywhere with us—that's why he's a
little bit tattered!"

Jess was already inside the enclosure,
but instead of her normal zookeeper's
uniform, she was dressed in a blue wet
suit. She waved when she saw Zoe and
Lucy approaching. She was sitting on the

edge of the saltwater pool with her legs
dangling in the water, watching Nina
and Alex swim along together.

Jess reached into a bucket next to the
pool, scooped up a handful of small silver
fish, and let them drop into the water.
As the fish sank to the bottom of the
pool, the twins rolled forward and
plunged underwater, chasing after them.

"Look how good they are at diving for food," called Jess, smiling.

Zoe could tell that Olivia loved the adorable little otters. She was staring at them, her eyes wide and excited. Then Olivia caught sight of Sasha, perched on a rock at the edge of the pool, and gasped.

"That's Sasha! She's cute, isn't she?" Zoe said.

"Can I hold her?" Olivia asked eagerly.

"Well, we don't usually pick up the wild animals because they aren't used to it and might not like it," Zoe explained gently. "Anyway, you're busy holding Eddie and you wouldn't want to put him down on the ground. He might get wet!"

Olivia nodded in agreement and gave Eddie a hug.

Zoe looked back at Sasha and thought she seemed a little bit sad. "Has Sasha tried diving for food yet?" she asked Jess, walking over to the pool.

"Not yet," replied Jess. "We'll need to bottle-feed her for a bit longer, until she's a stronger swimmer and feels more at home here. We can definitely help her with her swimming though—in fact, now that you're here, we can give her a special lesson! First of all, you'll need this."

Jess reached behind her and pulled out a bag tied with a ribbon. She passed it to Zoe, who opened it up carefully. "Your great-uncle asked me to buy it specially for you!" added Jess.

A thrill of excitement went through Zoe as she pulled out a ball of stretchy, shiny blue material. "A wet suit, just like yours!"

she exclaimed, unrolling the material and holding it up. "But it's the perfect size for me! Can I put it on now?"

"As long as your mom says it's OK," said Jess, glancing at Lucy. "You've got some guests, right?"

"No problem!" Zoe's mom replied, smiling. "I bet your cousin would love to see your special suit, Zoe. What a lovely present, huh? I'll help you put it on though. Wet suits can be really tricky if you're not used to them."

"You can get changed in the equipment room," said Jess, nodding to a small wooden shed at the edge of the enclosure. "I hope it fits!"

Inside the room, Zoe wriggled out of her clothes and pulled the wet suit over her feet. "Actually, I think it's too small for me!" she gasped, struggling to squeeze the stretchy fabric over her legs. "I need a bigger size!"

"No, you don't! That's how wet suits are supposed to fit, Zoe," her mom explained as she helped Zoe wriggle into the rubbery suit. "They're always tight. That's how they keep you warm when you're spending lots of time in cold water. They trap a very thin layer of water between

the suit and your body, which warms up
and keeps you nice and toasty."

With a final wriggle from Zoe, her
mom zipped up the back of the suit.
"There, you're all ready!"

Zoe couldn't wait to get started. She
was going to swim with three adorable
baby otters! But when she stepped back
outside the shed, she saw that Jess, Auntie
Carol, and Olivia had been joined by a
new person in the enclosure—Mr. Pinch,
the grumpy zoo manager.

"What's going on?" Mr. Pinch asked
with a frown. "I heard that some new
animals had arrived at the zoo, so I've
come to make sure everything is under
control. I didn't expect to see so many
people here!"

"Oh, I hope we're not causing any

trouble," said Auntie Carol.

"Mr. Pinch, this is my sister and my niece," Zoe's mom explained. "They're just visiting the zoo for a few days and wanted to see the new arrivals."

"Well, I hope the children aren't getting in the way," Mr. Pinch muttered, throwing a grumpy glance at little Olivia. "If they make any mess, no doubt I will be the one who has to clean it up!"

Zoe managed to hold her tongue, but she heard an angry chatter from Meep. Mr. Pinch always grumbled about

Zoe wandering around the zoo, saying
that only *real* zookeepers should work
with the animals, not children. Zoe
thought this was very unfair, since she
always tried her best to help out. Still,
she never argued back. When Great-
Uncle Horace was away, Mr. Pinch was
officially in charge of the zoo.

"Perhaps we'd better take Olivia back
to the cottage and find her a snack?"
Zoe's mom suggested, and Auntie Carol
nodded. "We'll start on dinner too. But
Zoe does have a special job to do here,
Mr. Pinch, so I hope you don't mind if she
stays for a little while."

"She'll be doing me a big favor,
Mr. Pinch!" added Jess, smiling at Zoe.

Just then, the walkie-talkie attached
to Mr. Pinch's uniform crackled. "Mr.

Pinch, come in, please!" came the voice
of David, who worked in the elephant
enclosure. "There's a lady here from the
local paper, looking for you. She wants
to run a story about some of our newer
arrivals. Can you come and speak to
her?"

"Oh, very well. As if I'm not busy
enough!" Mr. Pinch groaned, and
marched off in the direction of the
elephant enclosure.

"Phew!" chuckled Jess. "That should
keep Mr. Pinch busy for a little while!"

Once Zoe's mom and Auntie Carol had
taken Olivia back to the cottage, Zoe sat
down by the edge of the pool with Jess,
who showed her how to slowly ease her
legs into the water and get used to the
chilly temperature. Finally, Jess counted

to three, and Zoe took a deep breath and jumped in. She was a good swimmer, but the cold water only came up to her chest, so she could easily touch the bottom of the pool. As the cold water rushed inside her wet suit, she kicked her legs hard to get warm. Immediately, Nina and Alex wriggled over to her, and Zoe laughed as they nuzzled up to her with their whiskery noses. She heard a little squeak behind her, turned, and saw that Sasha was jumping in too!

"That's a good sign!" called Jess. "Sasha seems interested in you, Zoe; as soon as you got in the pool, she wanted to come swimming too! Stay close to her so she feels safe and supported. She might also like to try floating on her back."

Sasha paddled close to Zoe, her fur

sticking up in funny spikes and tufts. Zoe
started swimming slowly around the pool,
all the time checking that Sasha was still
with her. When Jess went to get some
toys for the otters to play with, Zoe took
the opportunity to whisper to the tiny

pup. "You're doing so well!" she said. "Do
you want to try diving underwater?"

Sasha squealed in agreement and
plunged her head under the surface,
wriggling her body. But she couldn't
get very far and quickly came back up,
spluttering and squeaking frustratedly.
"That's OK, Sasha. Every time you
try it, you'll get better and better," Zoe
reassured her.

Sasha squeaked again, hopefully this
time, and nodded her little head at the

plastic bucket on the side of the pool. "You want me to get you a fish?" asked Zoe.

Right at that moment, Alex and Nina popped their heads out of the water, each of them holding a shiny silver fish in their teeth. Sasha gave a sad little wail. "Sasha, what's wrong?" Zoe asked anxiously. "Why are you so upset?"

Sasha nuzzled against Zoe for a cuddle and gave a tiny squeak. "Oh, Sasha! That's not true. Alex and Nina aren't better than you—they're just older," explained Zoe. "They've had much more time to practice swimming and diving. I promise you'll be able to do those things just as easily as them, but you have to be a little patient."

Sasha gave another sad squeak, and Zoe shook her head. "You shouldn't be embarrassed of your spiky fur!" she said. "I know Alex's and Nina's fur is very soft and sleek, but I'll tell you a secret—I think yours is much nicer. It's a little like my hair—look! My curls stick up too!"

But Sasha still seemed downhearted, and when Jess arrived back at the pool with her arms full of balls to play with, the little pup wriggled out of the pool and huddled down on a rock by herself. Zoe felt awful for her new friend. *I'm going to help Sasha in any way I can*, she thought to herself. *But how?*

Chapter Five
Mr. Pinch's Plan

"But I don't *want* to go to sleep!"

It was Tuesday evening and Zoe was helping Auntie Carol get Olivia ready for bed—but it was turning out to be more difficult than Zoe had imagined! Olivia had put on her polka-dot pajamas, drunk her cup of warm milk, and brushed her teeth, but she did not want to go up to bed—no matter how hard Auntie Carol and Zoe tried to persuade her.

"Zoe can stay up late! Why can't I?" she complained, stamping her little feet on the kitchen floor. "I'm a big girl too!"

Zoe held out her hand and smiled at her little cousin. "Yes, you are! And when you're even bigger, you'll be able to stay up a little later, like me. Come on, let's go up to your bedroom together," she suggested. "We can choose a story and I'll read it to you! And Eddie can listen too," she added, picking up Olivia's tattered teddy from the floor, where Olivia had thrown him.

Olivia flung Eddie straight back down again, only just missing Meep. Zoe tried not to laugh as the little lemur scampered quickly to the kitchen window and hid behind the curtain, his angry little face peeping out. "I'm staying right here until Olivia goes to bed!" he squeaked firmly.

"I don't want a story!" grumbled Olivia. "I want to stay up!"

Auntie Carol sighed, but Zoe suddenly had an idea. "OK, Olivia!" she replied, smiling. "You can stay up. In fact, you're not allowed to go to bed! Not until you've played a special game with me. How does that sound?"

Olivia's face lit up and she nodded.

"First of all, you have to do ten jumping jacks!" Zoe told her. "I'll count. Ready? One ... two ... three ..."

Giggling, Olivia reached her hands up in the air and started jumping. "Next I want you to twirl around in a circle three times!" said Zoe. "Then tell me your ten favorite colors . . . And then do a somersault along the hallway carpet!"

Auntie Carol watched, chuckling, as Olivia followed Zoe's instructions, her tongue sticking out in concentration.

By the time she had touched her toes three times, the little girl was yawning sleepily and seemed to have forgotten all about her tantrum earlier.

"Thanks, Zoe," whispered Auntie Carol as she carried Olivia upstairs to the spare bedroom. "That worked perfectly!"

Once Olivia was sleeping, Zoe sat down at the kitchen table to eat dinner with her mom and Auntie Carol. As her mom served the lasagna, she smiled at Zoe. "Jess tells me you're doing a fantastic job with the otters—especially Sasha. It sounds like they're settling in really well, just in time for the first special show."

"What show?" asked Zoe.

"Oh, I thought Jess would have mentioned it," said Lucy. "Well, it comes from an idea Mr. Pinch had last week."

Zoe made a face at the mention of the zoo manager. "Come on now, Zoe!" her mom went on. "I know Mr. Pinch can be difficult sometimes, but this *is* a good idea. It's to help the zoo make a little bit more money. Every month, we'll choose a different animal to be the zoo's special focus. We'll put up posters, sell toys and books about those animals in the gift shop, and put on a show twice a day where the zookeeper tells the visitors all about that animal. Mr. Pinch thought that the sea otters could be the first special animals, seeing as they're our newest arrivals. The first show's going to be in a few days' time."

Zoe had to admit that a special show sounded great—but she wondered if picking the sea otters first was such a good idea. Sasha was already finding it hard to keep up with the twins. How would she cope with a huge audience watching her?

On Thursday, Zoe raced home from school so that she could watch the very first show at the otter enclosure. Meep was waiting for her at the zoo entrance, perched on the carved wooden gates as usual.

"It's starting right now, Zoe!" he chirped eagerly.

Jess had put up signs directing visitors to the right place, showing a beautiful photograph of the new sea otters, and a crowd was already gathering next to the fence. Everyone was chatting eagerly. "Aren't they adorable?" said one lady, snapping a picture on her camera.

Zoe stood on her tiptoes to see better, and Meep perched on her head. Nina and Alex were splashing through their saltwater pool, gliding on their backs together, then racing to get the fish that Jess threw into the water for them. Jess was speaking into a special microphone attached to her shirt collar, telling the crowd all about the otters. "As you can see, the twins love swimming!" she said. "Sea otters love the water. In fact, in the wild, sea otters can spend their whole lives in the water. Imagine that!"

Zoe craned her neck to try to catch a

glimpse of the littlest otter. Sasha was
in the pool too, and doing her best to
keep up, but Zoe could see that she was
struggling. The pup was slower than the
twins, and couldn't reach any of the balls

or fish before them. Her tufty fur was
messy and spiky compared to their
sleek, shiny coats, and she seemed
to quickly grow tired from all the
swimming. Across the crowd, Zoe
saw Mr. Pinch standing with his
hands on his hips and a frown
on his face.

When Jess announced that the show
was finished, the crowd clapped and
wandered off, talking eagerly about the
beautiful otters. Quickly, Zoe slipped
inside the enclosure and rushed over to
Sasha, who was sitting in a miserable
furry huddle all by herself. When Sasha
saw Zoe, she gave a sad squeak.

"It doesn't matter that you're not as quick as Nina and Alex yet," Zoe told her gently. "You're still doing really well!"

Nina and Alex swam up to their sister and squeaked encouragingly at her. "Your big brother and sister think so too, see?" said Zoe, smiling at the twins. "They're right—you just need a little bit more practice, and soon you'll be able to do everything they do. And we'll all help you!"

Nina squeaked in agreement and Alex nuzzled right up to Sasha. Zoe could tell that both of the older otters wanted to cheer their little sister up—and by the time she and Meep said good-bye to them all, Sasha *did* seem a little happier. But as Zoe left the enclosure, she overheard Mr. Pinch grumbling at Jess. "We need *all* the animals to put on a good show," he muttered. "That little one can't keep up!"

Jess nodded reluctantly. "Well, she is younger than the twins. . ." she said.

"We have to keep the little otter out of the show until she's as big and strong as the others," Mr. Pinch told her.

"Oh no," whispered Zoe to Meep as Mr. Pinch marched off. "If Mr. Pinch isn't going to let Sasha take part anymore, she's going to be so upset!"

How would the little otter build her confidence if she wasn't allowed to participate in the show?

Chapter Six
Zoe's Training Tricks

After school on Friday, Zoe met Meep at the gates and they ran straight to the cottage. Auntie Carol and Olivia were doing an animal jigsaw puzzle at the kitchen table as they burst through the door. "Hi, Zoe! How was school today?" Auntie Carol called. "We had such a nice day. Olivia met the llamas!"

"Oh, good!" replied Zoe, swapping her book bag for a small backpack hanging on the back of the kitchen door. "I've just come home to grab my wet suit," she explained, patting the backpack. "I'm going to help Sasha."

"Good luck!" Auntie Carol smiled as Zoe dashed back outside.

Zoe and Meep raced to the sea otter enclosure, darting through the busy crowds.

"Hi, Zoe!" called Jess from the saltwater pool. She was standing in the shallow end, watching Nina and Alex swim. "Put your wet suit on and jump in!"

Zoe got changed in the equipment room. She was getting a little more used to putting her wet suit on now, though it was still tricky to wriggle into it! She put her hair up in a ponytail and joined Jess in the water. Nina and Alex splashed over to her and greeted her by nuzzling their whiskery noses against her body, and she gave them a cuddle back. "Where's Sasha?" she asked Jess.

There was a squeak as Sasha popped her head out from behind one of the wooden ramps that ran around the enclosure. "Sasha hasn't seemed very eager to get in the water today," Jess explained. "In fact, after her bottle of milk at lunchtime, she hasn't jumped into the pool once! I wondered if she might be tired—she's had a lot to take in over the last few days."

"Maybe she's feeling upset about how the show went last night," Zoe whispered to Meep, who was perched on a rock by the edge of the pool, taking care not to let any water splash his fur. Meep was friends with lots of water-loving animals, but he preferred to stay nice and dry! "Let's go and talk to her."

Zoe climbed out of the pool and went to sit with Sasha, who squeaked sadly at her. "What's wrong, Sasha?" Zoe asked. She listened as Sasha explained how things had changed since the otters had arrived at the zoo. When they'd been in the wild, the twins had taken care of Sasha and caught fish for her, but now they were too busy having fun and she felt really left out. When she was sure that Jess was distracted by Nina and Alex, Zoe said quietly, "Sasha, I need to tell you something. Mr. Pinch thinks it might be better if just Nina and Alex perform in the next show."

The little otter gave another sad squeak.

"I know that makes you feel sad," Zoe said, seeing the little pup's face fall and her big dark eyes widen. "But *I* know you can do everything your sister and brother can, with just a little practice. Why don't you come into the pool with me and go for a swim?"

At first Sasha looked unsure, but eventually the little pup agreed. Zoe climbed back into the pool and waited for Sasha to splash in next to her. "Jess, would it be OK if I used one of these rings?" Zoe asked, nodding toward a stack of brightly colored plastic rings on the side of the pool. "I want to see if Sasha would like to dive for it!"

"Of course, Zoe," said Jess, handing one over.

Zoe lifted up the ring, then let it drop from her hand and into the water. Sasha looked nervous, but rolled forward and plunged under.

Zoe crossed her fingers hopefully, but her heart sank as Sasha surfaced almost immediately, leaving the ring to sink right to the bottom of the pool. The little otter gave a frustrated squeal and shook her head. Zoe frowned as Sasha explained what the problem was. "You're worried you're going to get lost under the water?" she whispered back. "I promise that won't happen, Sasha—I'm here watching you the whole time! You've just lost your confidence, that's all. Let's try it again."

But Sasha was getting more and more upset—and to make matters worse, Nina and Alex had just caught some fish that Jess had thrown for them and were turning happy flips in the water to celebrate! Sasha gave a jealous, sulky squeak, turning her back on her big brother and sister.

Suddenly, Zoe realized something. *This is just how Olivia was behaving last night when she wanted to stay up late like me! What if I distract Sasha with a fun game and see if that makes her feel happier?*

"Listen, Sasha," whispered Zoe, hoping her idea would work. "How would you like to eat a nice shiny fish just like Nina and Alex?"

Sasha's eyes lit up and she nodded. "OK, then!" replied Zoe. "You can have a fish— but you have to dive for it. We'll go right to the shallowest end of the water, and I'll stay with you the whole time, I promise."

Sasha hesitated, and Zoe could see the little pup thinking it through. She didn't want to try diving again, but she was eager to have a fish like the twins! To

Zoe's delight, Sasha wriggled her furry
little body to the shallowest part of the
pool, where Zoe could kneel down in the
water. Zoe grabbed a silver fish from the
bucket at the side of the pool.

"I've got an idea! I'll count to three,
and when you dive, I'll put my hand
underwater too, and point to where the
fish is," Zoe explained. "All you have to
do is follow my hand! OK?"

Meep had scampered around the pool
to sit closer to Zoe and Sasha. "And I'll
cheer for you, Sasha!" the little lemur
chirped warmly.

Sasha nodded, but she looked really
nervous.

"Ready?" said Zoe. "I'm going to drop
the fish *now*—there it goes! And on the
count of three, dive and follow my hand!

One . . . two . . . three!"

Sasha stuck her head under the water and gave a wriggle and a push. Zoe kept her hand very close to the little otter's head so that Sasha could see it clearly and be guided through the water. Down they went, and just a moment later, Sasha caught the fish with her teeth. Quickly, Zoe lifted her hand out of the water and Sasha followed, popping up with a splash and a triumphant squeal.

"You see?" said Zoe, smiling as Sasha gobbled up the fish. "That wasn't so hard, was it? I think you could give that one more try, but this time we'll move to an area of the pool that's a little deeper. OK?"

The little pup was so excited that she'd managed to catch the fish, she agreed

immediately. Zoe went and grabbed
another fish, then she took two steps
toward the deeper end and dropped it.
"One . . . two . . . three!" she said.

Sasha got to the fish even more quickly this time, following Zoe's hand right to the bottom of the pool. "Excellent!" said Zoe, grinning. "You definitely earned that fish, Sasha. I knew you could do it!"

From the far side of the pool, Zoe heard clapping. Looking across, she saw that Jess was applauding! "Well done, Zoe!" she called. "You're doing so well. It's almost as though Sasha understands everything you're saying to her. Maybe the sound of your voice is soothing her. Either way, it's working!"

Smiling to herself, Zoe clambered out of the pool and scooped up another tiny silver fish from the bucket, which she held out for Sasha. The little pup gobbled it down, her eyes wide with excitement.

Zoe smiled at the little otter pup. "We'll

do some more swimming tomorrow, and I promise you can have some more fish then," she whispered to Sasha.

Meep sighed. "Seeing Sasha enjoying a snack is making me feel hungry!"

Zoe giggled. Meep was *always* hungry! As she walked home for dinner with the little lemur perched on her shoulder, Zoe felt tired but happy. "I really think little Sasha's doing much better now, don't you?" she said, reaching up to tickle Meep's fluffy belly.

Meep squeaked in agreement, though Zoe could tell he was already distracted by the thought of dinner. She was pleased she could help the young sea otter, even if Sasha couldn't take part in the show yet . . .

"Remember, today's show starts at three o'clock!" Zoe reminded her mom as she laced up her sneakers.

"I wouldn't miss it for anything, Zoe. Auntie Carol and Olivia will be there too," her mom promised.

It was Saturday, and Zoe was leaving to help Jess get the sea otter enclosure ready for the show. She'd been busy all morning with her homework, then feeding the monkeys and the hippos their breakfast, but now that the show was almost here, she was feeling jittery and nervous. She knew that Nina and Alex would perform brilliantly for the crowd—but she was worried that Sasha might still get upset seeing her big brother and sister being the stars, when she wasn't even allowed to take part. *If she does get upset today, at least Meep and I will be there to cheer her up*, she told herself.

Jess was sweeping inside the enclosure when Zoe arrived and used her special necklace to open the gate. "Zoe, if you could grab that spare broom and help me finish this off, that would be amazing!" she called. "Then we'll need to stock up on fresh fish and make sure the saltwater levels and temperature of the pool are ready for the show. Mr. Pinch will be coming around to watch again today. It'll be great to show him how well the otters are doing!"

Zoe got to work right away. There were always plenty of jobs to help out with at the Rescue Zoo, and she loved being involved—even if it was hard work sometimes! Jess was humming cheerfully as they completed their tasks, and Zoe found herself joining in. She was even happier to see Sasha splashing in the water with her brother and sister, following them when they dived, even though she couldn't manage to swim as deeply as they could. "I think our practice yesterday really helped Sasha!" she said to Jess.

The otter-keeper smiled. "Yes, she's doing so much better today, isn't she?"

Zoe saw Sasha's little ears prick up.

Eagerly, the little pup paddled toward
the edge of the pool and squeaked
hopefully up to Zoe.

Zoe's heart sank. The little otter was
asking if she'd be able to take part in
today's show—but Zoe knew she couldn't.
She felt sure that Mr. Pinch wouldn't have
changed his mind.

When Jess was busy in the equipment
room, Zoe found a moment to crouch
down next to the pool and speak to
Sasha. "I'm sorry, Sasha," she said gently.
"You're doing really well, like Jess said,
but Nina and Alex will do this show by
themselves, and hopefully you can join in
next time."

As Sasha's face fell, Nina and Alex
squeaked kindly and encouragingly at
their little sister, telling her not to be

upset or worried. Zoe bent down and
scooped the tiny otter out of the water,
and wrapped her in a big, fluffy towel to
warm her up. "Let's get you dry, and then
we can pick a nice spot on the rocks to
sit and watch the show,"
she suggested quietly.
"Even if you can't
be in it, you can
still enjoy it!
And you'll
be able to
have a good
look at
everybody
in the
crowd—I
always think
that's lots of fun."

By the time the crowd started to
assemble on the other side of the fence,
the enclosure was looking spick-and-span,
with a bucket full of fresh fish by the
water's edge. Jess had attached the special
microphone to her shirt and the twins
were gliding through the water together.
Zoe sat with Sasha curled up next to
her and Meep perched on her shoulder.
"Look, there's your mom and Auntie
Carol and Olivia—and Great-Uncle
Horace!" the little lemur squeaked.

Zoe smiled and waved as her family
took their places next to the fence, Olivia
clutching her tattered teddy. "Great-
Uncle Horace, you're back!" Zoe called.
"Did you find the special swans you were
looking for?"

Great-Uncle Horace was beaming.

"I did!" he called. "Wonderful, elegant creatures! But I'm absolutely thrilled to be home in time to watch our newest arrivals in action. I hear you've been doing a splendid job here, Zoe!"

Just then, they heard Jess's voice come over the loudspeakers.

"I think it's time to start!" she announced, holding up a bright-yellow ball. "Thank you for coming, everyone. I'm very happy to introduce twins Nina and Alex, who are a year old. They are our newest animals at the Rescue Zoo, so please give them a warm welcome!"

The crowd chattered excitedly as the otters began swooping and diving, chasing after the fish and turning somersaults. Zoe glanced over at the

audience and grinned to see Auntie Carol
lifting a wide-eyed Olivia right up to
the fence so that she could see better. The
little girl chuckled and pointed as the
baby otters tumbled through the water.

I wish Sasha could have taken part, thought
Zoe, looking down at the tufty little otter
sitting beside her, *but at least everyone's
enjoying the show—and this time there's
nothing for Mr. Pinch to get mad about!*

Suddenly, Zoe heard a familiar, anxious
wail from the crowd. "Eddie!"

She looked over again and saw Olivia
reaching desperately over the side of the
fence. "Mommy, I dropped Eddie in the
water!" she whimpered, tears beginning
to stream down her face.

Zoe peered into the deepest part of
the pool, right by the fence. She could

just make out a blurry shape, sinking deeper and deeper: Olivia's precious teddy bear, Eddie. Olivia started to cry louder, and there was a murmur throughout the crowd. Zoe heard Mr. Pinch grumble, "What is going on?"

Then Zoe noticed a sudden movement next to her—a fuzzy blur shuffled quickly toward the pool and leaped in with a little splash. Zoe realized what was happening, just as a man in the crowd called out, "Look! There's another baby otter—an even smaller one!"

Chapter Seven
Sasha Saves the Day!

"Sasha!" cried Zoe. The little pup had scampered down from her seat and splashed into the pool! The crowd gasped, and Zoe held her breath as Sasha glided through the water. She swam right past where her brother and sister were performing and disappeared under the surface with a wriggle and a splash.

A moment later, her tufty head popped back up, dripping with water and with fur sticking up everywhere. Her black eyes gleamed happily as she showed the crowd what she was carrying in her teeth.

"Eddie!" yelled Olivia. "She's got Eddie!"

Sasha swam to the side of the pool with a very soggy teddy bear, and Jess bent down and gently took Eddie from her. She gave him a careful squeeze so that most of the water trickled out, and then leaned over the fence and handed him back to Olivia, who hugged him tight. "Eddie!"

Suddenly, the whole crowd was laughing and cheering, chattering about the clever little otter and snapping pictures. "That has to be the cutest thing I've ever seen!"

Zoe heard a teenage girl with long red hair tell her friend. "A beautiful baby otter rescuing a teddy bear!"

"I filmed it all on my phone!" her friend told her. "I can't wait to show everyone at school. They'll all want to come and see her!"

Zoe glanced over at Mr. Pinch. The grumpy zoo manager's expression had changed completely. He was beaming from ear to ear and nodding along with the rest of the crowd. "Of course, this special show was all my idea," he explained loudly to whoever would listen. "And it was my decision to feature *all* of the sea otters too. Very intelligent creatures. I just knew they'd be popular!"

"Zoe, look!" chirped Meep, pointing. "All the otters are swimming together!"

Zoe turned back to the pool—and grinned. Nina and Alex had both offered their little sister a furry paw, and all three were floating along on their backs, with Sasha in the middle. From the cheerful squeals and squeaks she was letting out, Zoe could tell she was very happy. Eagerly, she tried a somersault in the water—and although she didn't quite manage it and splashed water everywhere, the crowd seemed to love it. "They are all so adorable!" cried a blonde lady standing close to Mr. Pinch. "The scruffy little one is the cutest. I'd come back and watch her every day if I could."

"I can't believe it," whispered Zoe to Meep. "Sasha is the star of the whole show!"

When the show was over and the audience began trickling away, Zoe ran to give her mom and Great-Uncle

Horace a hug before they went back to the cottage. "You did such a good job helping Sasha gain her confidence, Zoe," said her mom, smiling. "I'm so proud of you."

"Hear, hear!" said Great-Uncle Horace.

Zoe shook her head. "It was all thanks to Sasha—and to Olivia!" she added, beaming at her little cousin, who giggled. "And to Eddie, of course!" and she patted the soggy teddy bear on the head.

"We'll have a special dinner tonight to celebrate," said Zoe's mom. "You'll come too, won't you, Uncle Horace?"

"Can I stay here for a little bit longer?" asked Zoe. "I want to help Jess finish cleaning up. I'll be home soon!"

Her mom agreed, and Zoe waved them off. Then she knelt by the side of the pool to talk to the youngest sea otter.

"Sasha, you were amazing!" she whispered. "You rescued Olivia's special teddy and you swam in front of everyone, just like Nina and Alex!"

Sasha nodded and squeaked back, her eyes bright. "I'm so glad you're feeling more confident," Zoe replied, smiling.

As Zoe and Meep left the enclosure a little bit later, Zoe turned back to glance over the fence one last time and grinned. The three otters were in the pool, all of them clasping paws again as they floated through the water. "Sasha seems really happy now, doesn't she, Meep?" Zoe said.

"So do Nina and Alex," chirped Meep. "And *I'm* really happy they've come to live at the Rescue Zoo with us, Zoe!"

"Me too, Meep," replied Zoe, cuddling her little friend. "I wonder what animal Great-Uncle Horace will bring home with him next time? I can't wait to find out!"

If you enjoyed Sasha's story,
look out for:

The cub blinked nervously at the crowd.
He opened his mouth to reveal a row of
white baby teeth and gave a squeaky
growl. His little paws trembled and he
looked very weak and frightened.

"Stand back, please!" Mr. Pinch
announced as the visitors pushed forward

to get a better look. "Make way for the vet."

Zoe's mom knelt down slowly next to the cub. "There, there, little one. I'm not going to hurt you," she soothed as she examined the lion's eyes, ears, teeth, tummy, and paws. The cub shrank away, snarling as fiercely as he could. Zoe's mom looked up. "You found him just in time, Uncle Horace. It looks like he hasn't eaten in weeks."

Zoe and Meep shared a worried look. The cub seemed confused and very scared. He kept turning his head from side to side, as if he was looking for someone in the crowd. Zoe desperately wanted to explain that everyone at the Rescue Zoo was really kind and wanted to help him. But she couldn't talk to him in front of the crowd—she had to keep the animals' secret.

Zoe felt a gentle tug on her hair, and realized it was Kiki trying to get her attention.

Great-Uncle Horace was standing next to her. Leaning closer, he whispered, "My dear, this little guy needs help. Will you promise to look after him for me?"

Zoe stared at her great-uncle and then nodded. "I promise. I'll try my very best to help the cub."

Great-Uncle Horace beamed at her. "That's my girl, Zoe! I know you can do it." He smiled brightly as Kiki nibbled his ear.

"OK!" he announced. "Let's see what's been going on around here while I've been gone. I must say hello to all the animals right away. First, a trip to visit Charles, I think. I do miss that old fellow when I'm on my travels. Did you know, everyone, that giant tortoises like Charles can live to be over two hundred years old? Incredible!" Great-Uncle Horace waved to the crowd, winked at Zoe, then strode off happily down the path toward the tortoise enclosure.

Kiki spread her wings and soared across to Zoe from Great-Uncle Horace's shoulder and circled over her head. Something light and soft floated down into Zoe's hand. It was one of Kiki's bright, beautiful blue tail feathers.

Zoe tucked it safely into her pocket. Kiki was Great-Uncle Horace's lucky charm, and it was almost as if the macaw was saying "Good luck!" to her. Great-Uncle Horace had asked her to help the little lion cub—and she was determined to keep her promise.

Once Great-Uncle Horace was out of sight, Zoe's mom clapped her hands together. "Let's get the cub to the zoo hospital," she called. "He needs food and water right away."

A zookeeper brought over a special blanket, which Zoe's mom gently wrapped around the frightened lion cub. She scooped him up and headed straight for the hospital, weaving her way through the chattering crowd.

Zoe knew the blanket would keep the animal toasty warm and would also protect her mom's hands from any scratches. She followed, with Meep scampering along beside her.

"Ahem!"

A bony finger tapped her on the shoulder. Zoe's heart sank as she turned to see Mr. Pinch glaring at her. Zoe noticed he still had a smudge of banana on his forehead.

"And just where do you think *you're* going?" he sneered.

"I was going to the hospital—" Zoe began.

Mr. Pinch narrowed his eyes. "Young lady, the hospital is for *zoo staff only*. Whenever Horace brings back a new arrival it creates lots of paperwork, and it's up to me to keep the zoo running smoothly. So I will *not* have an unruly little girl and a troublemaking lemur getting in the way!" he said, pointing at Meep.

Meep squeaked and made a very rude noise, as if to prove just how troublesome he could be.

Zoe nodded sadly. No matter how helpful she tried to be, Mr. Pinch always told her she was causing trouble. But as soon as Mr. Pinch was out of sight, an idea popped into her head.

"Don't worry, Meep," she whispered. "With Mr. Pinch busy at the hospital, we can tell the other animals all about the new arrival."

Suddenly, she felt much better!

NEW AT THE ZOO

Zoe Parker has an amazing secret—she can talk to animals!

Her special talent comes in handy at her great-uncle's Rescue Zoo. Here, injured or endangered animals find a safe place to live.